JESSICA
Jazzberries

Written by **Kailey Mae Robertson**

To order additional copies of this book, contact:
Xlibris Corporation
1-888-795-4274
www.Xlibris.com
Orders@Xlibris.com

The sun rose in the summer morning sky, drying the fresh dew from the grass. Jessica awakened to the sweet smell of pancakes which her mom faithfully made every Saturday morning.

"It's SATURDAY!" she screeched as she flung off her bed covers. Not only would there be delicious pancakes waiting for her, but Jessica's mom had promised they would go raspberry picking today. Raspberry picking was something that Jessica and her mother did every summer. Raspberries were Jessica's favorite food in the whole wide world! She loved the tangy sweetness that danced on her tongue when she popped them into her mouth.

Jessica gobbled up her pancakes as fast as she could and headed out the door, grabbing as many empty fruit baskets as she could carry in her little hands.

"Come on mom let's go!" she shouted over her shoulder as she ran to the car.

Her mother loved raspberry picking too. Leaving the dirty dishes behind, she grabbed the car keys, a bunch of fruit baskets, and… WOOSH…they were off to the Mc Fadden's berry farm.

In the back seat of the car, Jess rolled down the window. She loved the drive to the Mc Fadden's berry farm. The air was sweet and fresh. Jessica thought that maybe the breeze picked up the aroma of the raspberries because she was certain she could already smell them.

For miles and miles, Jessica could see rolling hills covered in berry bushes. Blackberries, blueberries, strawberries, and raspberries were just a few of the different berries that the McFadden's farm had to offer. If there was a berry you could think of, the Mc Fadden's Farm had them. They offered berries in baskets ready to eat or you could pick your own berries if you preferred. Jessica thought that picking berries was much more fun. Choosing her own perfect berry was an art that she had learned from her mom. Only the ripest, plumpest, juiciest berries made it into Jessica's basket.

There was only one problem. Bees! Jessica
didn't like bees. It seemed that every summer,
the bees were also busy selecting the biggest,
juiciest, yummiest berries because they were
always buzzing around the ones Jessica wanted. It
occurred to Jessica that she may have to share all
those berries with the bees if she ever expected to
enjoy their sweet honey on her pancakes.

Jessica and her mom drove up the dusty drive to
the Mc Fadden's farm. Old Lady Mc Fadden greeted
them as they arrived. "Welcome!" she said with
a big cheesy grin. "Make yourself at home. Go
anywhere you like in the fields and pick whatever
pleases you. Just let me know when you are ready
to leave.

Jessica bolted for the fields. She had a plan. For the best selection, she decided to pick berries where nobody had been. "Somewhere in the middle of the field between the blackberries and the raspberries" she thought.

So Jessica and her mom walked and walked for what seemed like forever. The berry canes were overgrown. Jess's arms and legs were getting scratched from the prickly thorns that poked themselves out into the open rows.

Jessica suddenly yelled, "STOP! Right here, mom! This is it! This is the place!" Jessica always had great luck in finding the best spots for berry picking. She called it her "berry-good instincts".

Without wasting a single second, Jessica plowed into the berry bush. There it was! Dark red, soft to the touch, and about as big as she could imagine a berry could be. It formed a perfect V-shape and was made up of many tiny little balls. Jessica's grandpa had told her that those tiny little balls were called drupelets. "Who makes up funny names like that?" Jessica thought. "They don't droop at all!"

She gently plucked the berry from its thorny vine and opened her mouth as wide as it could go. She placed it on her tongue and closed her mouth tight to let the zippy flavor spread over her taste buds as she squeezed it between the roof of her mouth and her tongue. "Yup! Perfection!" She beamed as she smacked her lips with satisfaction.

Jessica's mom had already filled one basket as Jess was busy savoring the moment. But now it was time to get down to business. Jess rolled up her sleeves and dived into the bushes, picking as many perfect berries as she could.

As the sun rose higher in the clear blue sky, the morning became very hot. Exhausted, Jessica laid down right in the middle of the row to have a rest. She opened her eyes toward the bright, blinding sun. Dangling above her was a berry more colorful and more vibrant than she could have ever imagined a berry to be. It appeared to have bold stripes of varying colors.

Jessica was sure it was the blazing sun that made it appear this way, but to sure, she rose up from her rest to see it more clearly.

Without a doubt this was absolutely amazing. A berry shaped like a raspberry, but striped like a rainbow! Blue, green, gold, pink, and red. Jessica counted the colors. One, two, three, four, five. Each color made a distinct line. There was no doubt about it. This must be a rainbow berry.

"JAZZZZY!" Jessica shouted.

"What's jazzy?" asked her mom from two rows away.

"This rainbow berry! Come see, mom!" Jess replied.

"Very funny!" Mom said sarcastically.

"Look!" Jess held up the berry as high as she could so her mom could get a glimpse of it. "Oh, my! That's incredible! Don't eat that!" called out her mom.

Looking around, Jess noticed that she was surrounded by rainbow berries! Each striped berry had its own special look. Not one was identical to another.

"Wow, mom! These are so jazzy! They must be called JAZZBERRIES!" she laughed.

Jessica and her mother filled all their baskets with the strange, beautiful berries without eating a single one. Jessica's grandpa had always taught them that some berries can be poisonous and to be extra careful when picking berries of any kind. "I wonder if grandpa has ever seen a jazzberry," Jessica wondered out loud.

Both Jess and her mother were anxious to get back to the Mc Fadden's farmhouse to see what type of berry they had packed into their baskets. While walking with their arms full of baskets, they talked about all of the wonderful things they could make with the colorful jazzberries.

"Jazzberry pie, jazzberry muffins, jazzberry upside down cake, jazzberry jam, jazzberry juice... the possibilities were endless.

Old Lady Mc Fadden greeted them upon their return from the scorching, hot fields and asked if they found everything they were looking for.

"Oh yes!" proclaimed Jessica. "We found what we were looking for and MORE! We found JAZZBERRIES!"

"Jazzberries?" questioned Lady Mc Fadden with a puzzled look on her face. Jessica held up the basket so the plump little lady could see.

"Oh my! Oh my goodness!" Mrs. Mc Fadden's jaw dropped. She covered her mouth as if to hide her surprise. "Where did you find these beautiful striped berries, my dear?" she asked. Jessica pointed to the middle of the field where she and her mom had been picking all morning.

"Goodness gracious! That's right in the area where many types of berries come together. Blueberries, blackberries, golden raspberries, pink raspberries, red raspberries, and gooseberries. They must have come together to make those beautiful, rainbow berries. How amazing!

"Well, I just don't know how much to charge you for those berries because they are not on the list. I guess you can have them for free since you are the one who discovered them!" laughed Mrs. Mc Fadden.

"What will you call them, Jessica?" she asked.

"JAZZBERRIES!" Jessica chirped as she skipped to the car, fully energized by the exciting new discovery.

During the car ride home, Jess and her mom excitedly shouted out other possibilities for the jazzberries.

"Jazzberry ice cream, jazzberry pudding, jazzberry jello, jazzberry slushies, jazzberry milk shake…"

Once they got home, Jessica and her mother had decided that these berries were far too special to put into any baked goods. So they sat on the front porch swing, sipped ice-cold lemonade, and ate Jessica's jazzberries one by one…

...right from the basket.

Edwards Brothers, Inc.
Thorofare, NJ USA
November 16, 2011